Cambridge Early Years

Learner's Book 1C

Alison Borthwick, Gill Budgell, Kathryn Harper,
Claire Medwell & Cherri Moseley

Contents

Note to parents and practitioners					3

Block 5: Who helps us?
Let's Explore					4
Communication and Language					8
Mathematics					20

Block 6: Let's move
Let's Explore					22
Communication and Language					26
Mathematics					38

Acknowledgements					40

Note to parents and practitioners

This Learner's Book provides activities and stories to support the third term of Let's Explore, Communication and Language, and Mathematics for Cambridge Early Years 1.

Activities can be used at school or at home. Children will need support from an adult. Additional guidance about activities can be found in the **For practitioners** boxes.

Some activities use stickers. The stickers can be found in the section in the middle of this book.

Stories are provided for children to enjoy looking at and listening to. Children are not expected to be able to read the stories themselves.

Children will encounter the following characters within this book. You could ask children to point to the characters when they see them on the pages, and say their names.

The Learner's Book activities support the Teaching Resource activities. The Teaching Resource provides step-by-step coverage of the Cambridge Early Years curriculum and guidance on how the Learner's Book activities develop the curriculum learning statements.

Hi, my name is Mia.

Find us on the front covers doing lots of fun activities.

Hi, my name is Gemi.

Hi, my name is Rafi.

Hi, my name is Kiho.

Block 5 Who helps us?

People that help us
Choose stickers and say.

Who uses this?
Match, say and act out.

For practitioners
Children identify the different objects. You may need to offer support with this, helping to explain what the objects are and what they do. Children then draw lines to match the objects together. Once all objects are matched, children then do actions as to how they would use these objects. Ask *Who in our community uses these objects to help us?*

Can you draw a house?
Draw and colour.

For practitioners

Children draw and colour a house. This can be from their imagination or a house they know. Talk about how they will do this before they begin. As they are working, ask children what they are doing and why. When children have completed their pictures, ask them questions about their house, prompting them to talk about how they have drawn parts of the house and what each part is.

All the people ... ran and ran.

They caught Dan,
the flying man.

Where is Dan?

Point and say.

Look at the pictures. Point to Dan and say where he is.

For practitioners

Encourage children to use the phrase from the text, *Over …*, as they point to each picture. Some children may recognise the rhyming couplets, such as *crane/train, trees/seas*.

Transport ABC

A

Ambulance action,
Ambulance action.
Siren blaring,
Watch the ambulance go!

B

Big Blue Balloon,
Big Blue Balloon.
Fire roaring,
Watch the balloon go!

C D

Cart with a Donkey,
Cart with a Donkey.
Mouth hee-hawing,
Watch the donkey cart go!

E F G

Extra-Fast Green go-kart,
Extra-Fast Green go-kart.
Tyres screeching,
Watch the go-kart go!

H I J

High up In the Jeep,
High up In the Jeep.
People looking,
Watch the jeep go!

K

Kayak,
Speedy Kayak.
Paddles dipping,
Watch the speedy kayak go!

L

Loaded Lorry,
Loaded Lorry.
Wheels rolling,
Watch the loaded lorry go!

M

Motorboat,
Shiny Motorboat.
Sea spray jetting,
Watch the motorboat go!

N

New car,
New car.
Engine quiet,
Watch the new car go!

O

Old car,
Old car.
Engine chugging,
Watch the old car go!

P Q

Pink Quad bike,
Pink Quad bike.
Engine buzzing,
Watch the quad bike go!

R S

Red Submarine,
Red Submarine.
Radar pinging,
Watch the submarine go!

T

Tractor,
Trailer behind the Tractor.
Mud squelching,
Watch the tractor go!

U

Underground train,
Underground train.
Tracks squealing,
Watch the underground train go!

V W

Very big Wheel,
Very big Wheel.
Pods turning,
Watch the big wheel go!

X Y

X on a yellow Yacht,
X on a yellow Yacht.
Sails flapping,
Watch the X-Yacht go!

Z

Zip wire,
Zip wire.
Weeeeeeeeeeeeee
eeeeeeeeeeeeeeee!
Watch us go!

Busy transport

Draw and say.

Draw transport pictures. Say the name for each thing you draw.

For practitioners
Children draw their own transport pictures on the transport landscape. Help them to talk about their own experiences as they draw, and prompt them to name the vehicles they draw.

Stickers for pages 4–5

Stickers for page 20

Stickers for page 21

Stickers for pages 22–23

Stickers for page 39

Plates of cookies

Stick and say.

Put 4 cookies on each plate.
Make each plate of cookies different.

For practitioners

Invite children to add cookies to the first plate. Ask *How will you make the next plate different?*
Invite children to talk about and describe the groups of 4 that they have made. For example, *this plate has 1 chocolate cookie and 3 lemon cookies. This plate has 2 chocolate cookies and 2 lemon cookies.*

Block 6 Let's move

Moving around
Choose stickers and say.

For practitioners
Children explore the picture and discuss what they can see. Children stick the matching pictures in place, e.g., boat to water. Talk about things in the picture that roll, float, fly, go up and down, and round and around. Encourage children to find Rafi in the picture.

Floating and sinking!
Draw and say.

For practitioners
Talk about *sink* and *float*, reminding children what these words mean if necessary. Children draw a boat on top of the water that is floating. They then find an item in the classroom that they think will sink. Allow children to test this out. If the object sank, then they can draw it under the water.

What can you find in your classroom?
Find, draw and talk.

This goes round and around.

This goes up and down.

For practitioners
Read each sentence and ask children to find objects in the classroom that move round and around and up and down. Ask children to show you the movements and say which box they will draw the object in and why.

Row, Row, Row Your Boat (traditional song)

Row, row, row your boat, *(rowing)*
Gently down the stream.
Merrily, merrily, merrily, merrily,
Life is like a dream. *(happy face)*

Row, row, row your boat, *(rowing)*
Gently down the stream.
If you see a crocodile,
Don't forget to scream!
(shocked face, scream)

Row, row, row your boat, *(rowing)*
Gently down the river.
If you see a polar bear,
Don't forget to shiver!
(shocked face, shiver)

Row, row, row your boat, *(rowing)*
Gently out to sea.
If you see a big blue whale,
Say hello from me!
(shocked face, wave)

Row, row, row your boat, *(rowing)*
Gently round the lake.
If you see a jelly fish,
Don't forget to shake.
(shocked face, shaking)

Row, row, row your boat, *(rowing)*
Gently to the shore.
If you see a dinosaur,
Don't forget to roar!
(shocked face, roar)

Rock, rock, rock your boat, *(rocking)*
Gently to and fro.
If you rock your boat too hard …
Into the water you'll go
Splash! *(shocked face as if falling in – and splash!)*

If you see a …

Listen and draw.

Listen to the rhyme.
Draw each animal when you hear it.

For practitioners
Children listen to the rhyming song and draw each animal as they hear it. Read each verse and pause to allow time for children to respond before singing or saying the next one. New ideas can also be added.

What do you see?

Point and say.

Point to each animal. Describe what you see.

For practitioners

Children look at the picture and say the names of the animals they can see. Encourage them to describe each of the animals. Ask questions to prompt children to use appropriate language, e.g., *Is it black or white? Where are its teeth? Does it have big feet or small feet? Where is the crocodile?* Remind children of the language in the rhyme, as appropriate.

Bear on a Bike by Stella Blackstone

Bear on a bike,
As happy as can be,
Where are you going, bear?
Please wait for me!

I'm going to the market,
Where fruit and flowers are sold,
Where people buy fresh oranges
And pots of marigold.

Bear on a raft,
As happy as can be,
Where are you going, bear?
Please wait for me!

I'm going to the forest,
Where fearsome creatures prowl,
Where raccoons play and bobcats snarl
And hungry foxes howl.

Bear in a steam train,
As happy as can be,
Where are you going, bear?
Please wait for me!

I'm going to the seaside,
Where children love to play,
Where young friends dig and race
And swim, while fishes dart away.

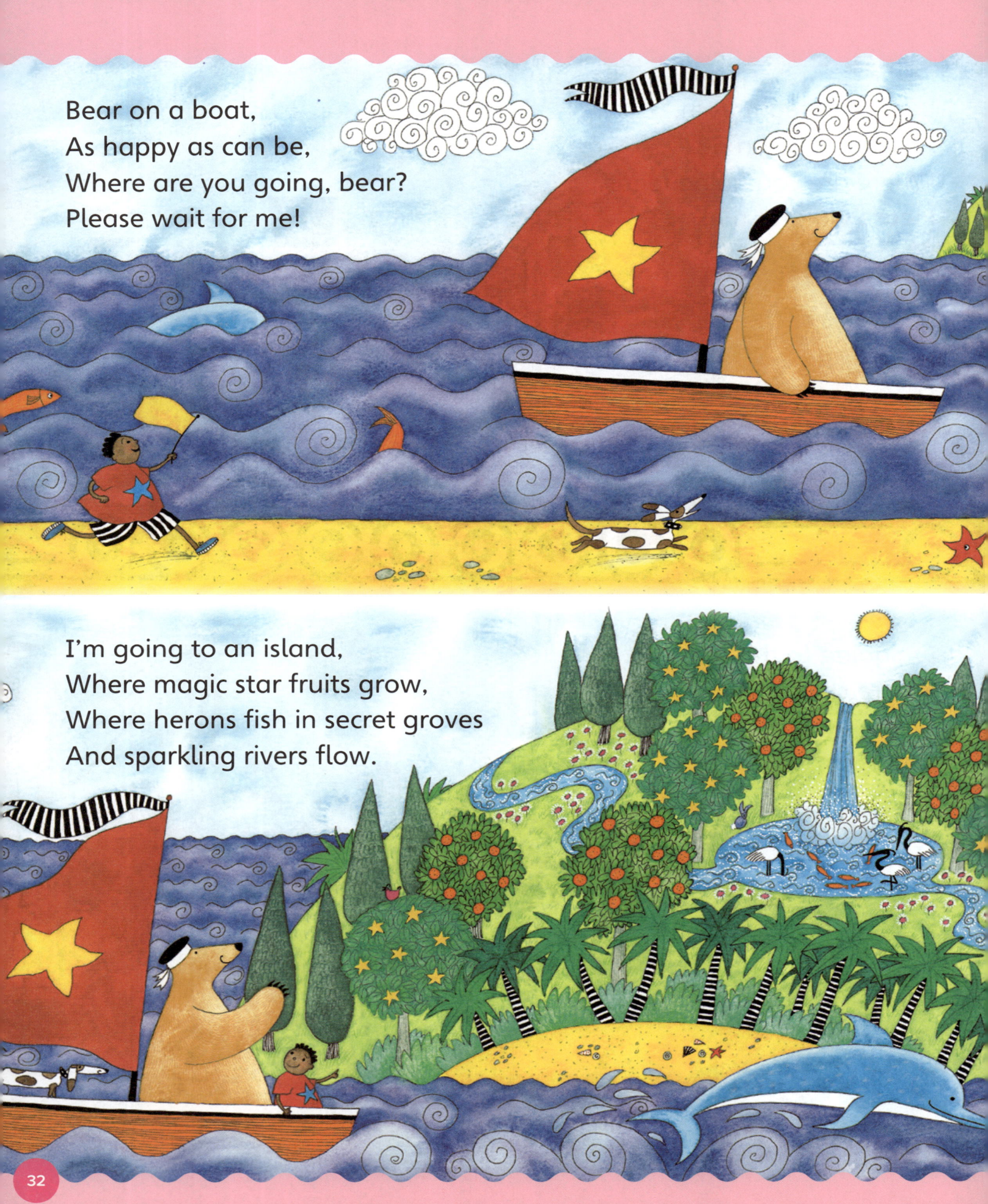

Bear on a boat,
As happy as can be,
Where are you going, bear?
Please wait for me!

I'm going to an island,
Where magic star fruits grow,
Where herons fish in secret groves
And sparkling rivers flow.

Bear in a carriage,
As happy as can be,
Where are you going, bear?
Please wait for me!

I'm going to a castle,
Where night is turned to day,
Where princes and princesses dance
And merry music plays.

Bear on a rocket,
Flying through the night,

Wherever you are going, bear,
Goodbye and goodnight!

Where is bear?

Look and say.

Look at each picture and say what bear is in or on.

For practitioners
Encourage children to say the phrase as they have heard it in the story text: *Bear on a . . . , Bear in a . . .*

What is bear on now?

Think and draw.

Draw bear on something different.
Say or write what he is on.

Bear on a _____.

For practitioners
Children will enjoy thinking of their own transport for bear. Some will draw and say; many will want to try to write in the space too. Support their writing as appropriate.

What is different?

Spot the difference.

Look at both of the pictures.
Find 5 differences.

For practitioners

Children look carefully at the two pictures to spot 5 differences and talk about them. Support them with intonation for statements and questions, as appropriate.

37

Ladybird doubles

Count and draw.

Draw the matching number of spots on the other wing case of each ladybird.

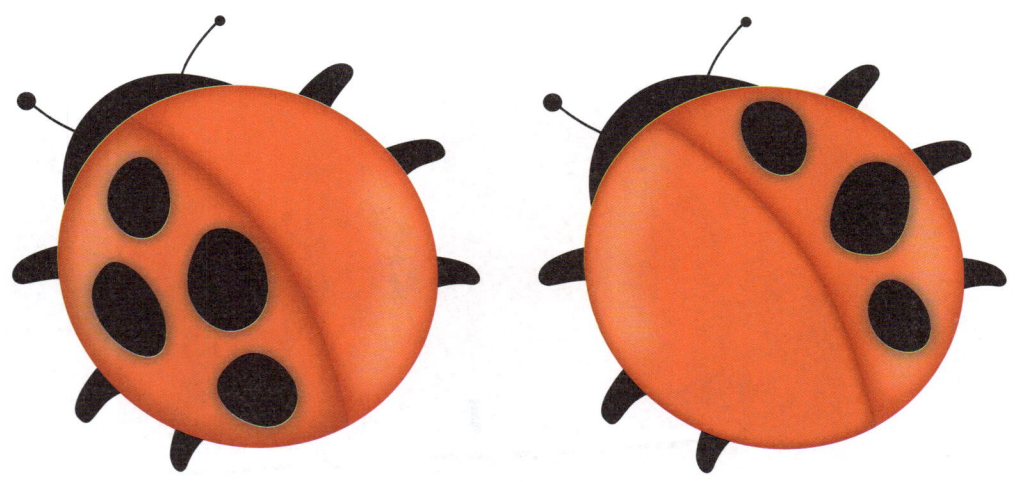

For practitioners

Invite children to talk about how each ladybird shows a double. Challenge children by asking questions such as *Which ladybird shows double 2? Do both sides match? Is there an equal number of spots on both sides?* Point to the spots and say *1 and another 1 is double 1*.

Share the fruit fairly
Choose stickers.

For practitioners
Encourage children to use the strategy of 'one for you, one for me' to share each set of fruit fairly between the two children.

Acknowledgements

The authors and publishers acknowledge the following sources of copyright material and are grateful for the permissions granted. While every effort has been made, it has not always been possible to identify the sources of all the material used, or to trace all copyright holders. If any omissions are brought to our notice, we will be happy to include the appropriate acknowledgements on reprinting.

Dan the Flying Man © Joy Cowley (Author), Annie Haywood (Illustrator) and published with kind permission by Clean Slate Press Ltd.

Bear on a Bike Text copyright © 1998 by Stella Blackstone. Illustrations copyright © 1998 by Debbie Harter. Used with permission from Barefoot Books, Ltd.

Thanks to the following artists at Beehive Illustration:
Laura Arias, Lays Bittencourt, Chloe Evans, Helen Graper, Tamara Joubert, Claire Philpott.

Cover characters by Becky Davies (The Bright Agency)